Fox
Gives Thanks

Written by Erin Rose Wage
Illustrated by John John Bajet

An imprint of Phoenix International Publications, Inc.
Chicago • London • New York • Hamburg • Mexico City • Sydney

Stepping softly through the wood
    there comes a fuzzy fox.
She crunches fallen leaves
    and hops along the mossy rocks.
Winter's on its way, thinks Fox.
    I'll need to fill my tummy.
So I will stuff this sack with
    any food I find that's yummy.

In the meadow fresh and sweet,
    Fox sniffs some juicy berries.
She spots some tasty acorns, too,
    and picks all she can carry.
This food will keep me fed, thinks Fox,
    through winter, cold and long.
Then she turns back toward the wood,
    whistling a winter song.

As Fox walks home, she meets
    a clever hedgehog by a brook.
He is busy counting feathers,
    and Fox stops to have a look.
"Why, Hedgehog," Fox declares,
    "I'd be home fast as fast can be…
If my sack were just as light
    as these feathers, one, two, three."

Fox ambles on and comes
across a mighty caribou.
She holds pumpkins with her antlers,
and some toadstools, red and blue.
"Oh, Caribou," says Fox, "I wish that
I were big and strong...
Although my heavy sack
feels lighter as I walk along."

When Fox stops next, she meets
    a brown squirrel digging in the ground.
And close to Squirrel sits a heap
    of acorns he has found.
"Squirrel, my friend," says Fox, "that hole
    seems damp and unprotected...
My trusty sack is the safest place
    for acorns I've collected."

Soon Fox hears a soft *kerplunk*
   and says, "What can that be?"
She gazes up and spies
   a raccoon resting in a tree.
"Hello, Raccoon," says Fox, "have you
   dropped something that you need?"
She shakes her head, so Fox treads on,
   pleased with her good deed.

By the time Fox reaches home,
    the moon is in the sky.
She finds her sack is strangely light…
    then heaves a heavy sigh.
My food has fallen out, thinks Fox.
    My day has been a waste!
Not one acorn nor one berry,
    not one teensy, tiny taste.

Suddenly, Fox hears a
    knock-knock-knocking at her door.
Her friends are here with all
    the food she dropped, plus even more!

"Welcome, friends," says Fox.
"Will you gather round my table?
As my way of giving thanks,
please eat all you are able!"

Published by PI Kids, an imprint of Phoenix International Publications, Inc.

8501 West Higgins Road, Suite 300
Chicago, Illinois 60631

PI Kids is a trademark of Phoenix International Publications, Inc.,
and is registered in the United States.
Printed in Canada/102023/CPC20231019

Paperback edition published in 2022 by Crabtree Publishing Company
ISBN 978-1-6499-6678-0 Printed in the United States of America

Customer Service: orders@crabtreebooks.com

Crabtree Classroom
A division of Crabtree Publishing Company
347 Fifth Avenue, Suite 1402-145
New York, NY, 10016

Crabtree Classroom
A division of Crabtree Publishing Company
616 Welland Ave.
St. Catharines, ON, L2M 5V6